SAMMY SPIDER'S
FIRST
TRIP TO ISRAEL

This **PJ BOOK** belongs to

_____

_____

JEWISH BEDTIME STORIES and SONGS

Sylvia Rouss

Illustrated by
Katherine Janus Kahn

KAR-BEN
PUBLISHING

May Israel find shalom with her neighbors.
—Sylvia Rouss
—Katherine Janus Kahn

KAR-BEN PUBLISHING
A division of Lerner Publishing Group, Inc.
241 First Avenue North
Minneapolis, MN 55401 U.S.A.
800-4KARBEN

Website address: www.karben.com

Library of Congress Cataloging-in-Publication Data

Rouss, Sylvia A.
    Sammy Spider's First Trip to Israel : a book about the five senses / by
Sylvia Rouss ; illustrated by Katherine Janus Kahn.
        p.   cm.
    Summary: Sammy Spider joins the Shapiro family on a vacation and he
uses his five senses to experience Israel.
    ISBN-13: 978–1–58013–035–6 (pbk. : alk. paper)
    ISBN-10: 1–58013–035–6 (pbk. : alk. paper)
    [1. Israel—Fiction. 2. Senses and sensation—Fiction.
3. Spiders—Fiction.] I. Kahn, Katherine, ill. II. Title
PZ7.R7622 Same 2002
    [E]—dc21   2002000931

Manufactured in the United States of America
1 – CG – 12/21/13

041420K2

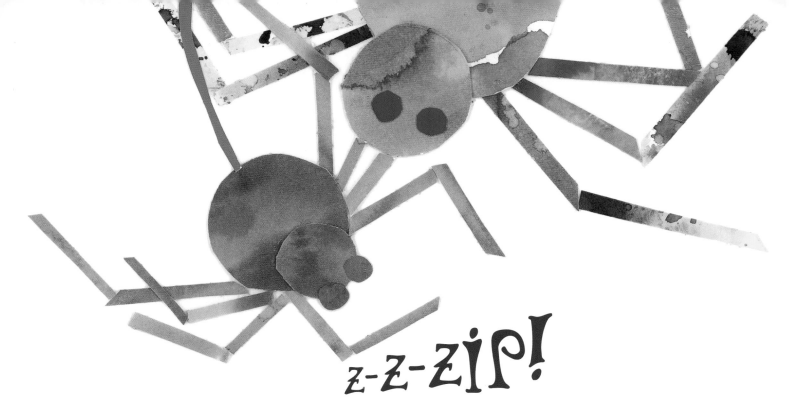

z-z-zip!

A curious Sammy Spider peered down from his web as Josh Shapiro closed his suitcase. "Mother," asked Sammy. "What is Josh doing?"

"He's packing for his family's trip to Israel," answered Mrs. Spider.

"Will we go too?" asked Sammy.

"Silly little Sammy," laughed Mrs. Spider. "Spiders don't fly to Israel. Spiders spin webs."

Sammy wasn't listening. He watched
Mr. Shapiro give Josh a toy airplane.
"Thanks!" exclaimed Josh. "Is this a model
of the El Al airplane that is flying us to Israel?"

"Yes," nodded Mr. Shapiro. "Now get your
suitcase, Josh. We're leaving
for the airport."

Sammy lowered himself on a strand of webbing to get a closer look at the little airplane. He had just crawled inside the window above the wing, when Josh picked up the airplane and dashed to the waiting taxi.

"Oh no!" cried Mrs. Spider as Josh ran out the door carrying the plane with Sammy inside. She was not sure what to do. Keeping Sammy from exploring was as hopeless as keeping the sun from rising each morning. And she knew he wouldn't be traveling alone.

From inside the little airplane, Sammy watched the big plane take off and fly above the clouds into the blue sky. He felt scared, but he couldn't help feeling a little bit excited, too.

Hours later, the plane landed at Ben Gurion Airport. A taxi took the Shapiros to their Tel Aviv Hotel.

"Shalom!" said the taxi driver as they got in.

"Shalom," replied Mr. Shapiro. "That's the Hebrew word for hello," he told Josh.

After they unpacked, the Shapiros decided to walk along the beach. Josh put on his swimsuit and grabbed the little plane.

"Shalom!" said the lifeguard.

"Shalom!" replied Josh.

Sammy smelled fresh sea air mingled with the aromas of sidewalk cafes and fruit stands. "I wish my mother were here to enjoy the smells of Israel," he thought.

That evening the family strolled along Dizengoff Street. Josh had the little plane tucked under his arm.

Shalom!" said a sidewalk musician who was playing Israeli music on his guitar.

Sammy loved the sounds of the busy street—people speaking Hebrew, car horns honking, and tourists bargaining with shopkeepers.

"I wish my mother could hear the sounds of Israel," thought Sammy.

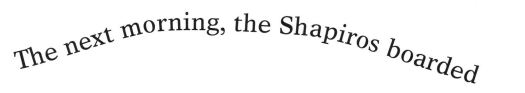

The next morning, the Shapiros boarded a bus for Jerusalem.

"Shalom!" said the bus driver.

The bus stopped for lunch at a kibbutz. "Many families live here together and farm the land," Mr. Shapiro told Josh as they gathered in the dining hall.

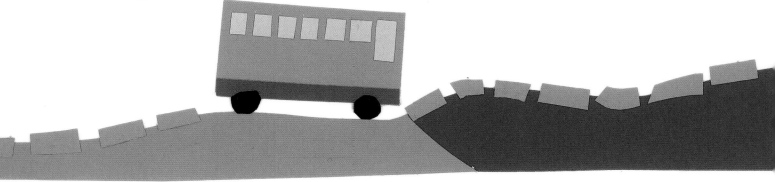

The Shapiros ate felafel, humus with pita, olives, and pickles. For dessert, they ate halvah.

Sammy was hungry, too. When everyone finished eating, he darted out of the little plane and sampled leftovers that had dropped to the floor. The pickles tasted sour, the olives salty, and the humus and felafel were spicy. Best of all was the sweet halvah.

Back inside the plane, Sammy thought, "I wish my mother were here to enjoy the tastes of Israel."

After lunch, Josh picked up his little plane and headed for the kibbutz farm. A cow grazing with her calf, and a hen clucking to her chicks reminded Sammy how much he missed his mother.

"Silly little Sammy," he could hear her say. "Have fun. I'll see you soon."

When the group reboarded the bus, the kibbutz families waved goodbye and shouted, "Shalom!"

"Shalom also means goodbye," Mrs. Shapiro told Josh.

The bus climbed the hilly road to Jerusalem. As they rounded a curve, the afternoon sun glistened off the stone buildings.

"We're here!" announced the bus driver.

"Wow! It looks like a golden city!" Sammy exclaimed to himself. "If only my mother could see Israel, too."

The bus reached the Old City. The Shapiros
got off and walked the narrow alleyways to
the Jewish Quarter.

"The Western Wall is all that
is left of the Holy Temple
in Jerusalem," the
guide explained.

"Shalom!" said the young soldier at the checkpoint.

"Shalom!" Josh replied. Josh and his father walked toward the wall.

Sammy saw some people praying. Others were tucking little notes between the huge stone blocks. "They have written special prayers," Mr. Shapiro told Josh.

Sammy crawled out of the little plane onto the wall. The huge stones felt hard and rugged. Yet in the cracks between them, Sammy noticed little plants were growing.

"It's just like the land of Israel," thought Sammy. "Hard and rugged, yet a special home to all Jews. I wish my mother were here to touch and feel Israel."

He wanted to tuck his own prayer in the wall, but he knew what his mother would say. "Silly little Sammy. Spiders don't write prayers, spiders spin webs." And that's exactly what he did.

The days passed quickly. The Shapiros traveled all over Israel, and Sammy went along, snug and safe in Josh's little plane.

They rode camels in the Negev desert, and Sammy felt the soft wool of the animals.

They snorkeled off the beaches of Eilat, and Sammy saw the **colorful fish**.

They stopped at a date
farm in the Galilee,
and Sammy tasted
the sweet fruit.

They floated in the Dead Sea,
and Sammy smelled the salty water.

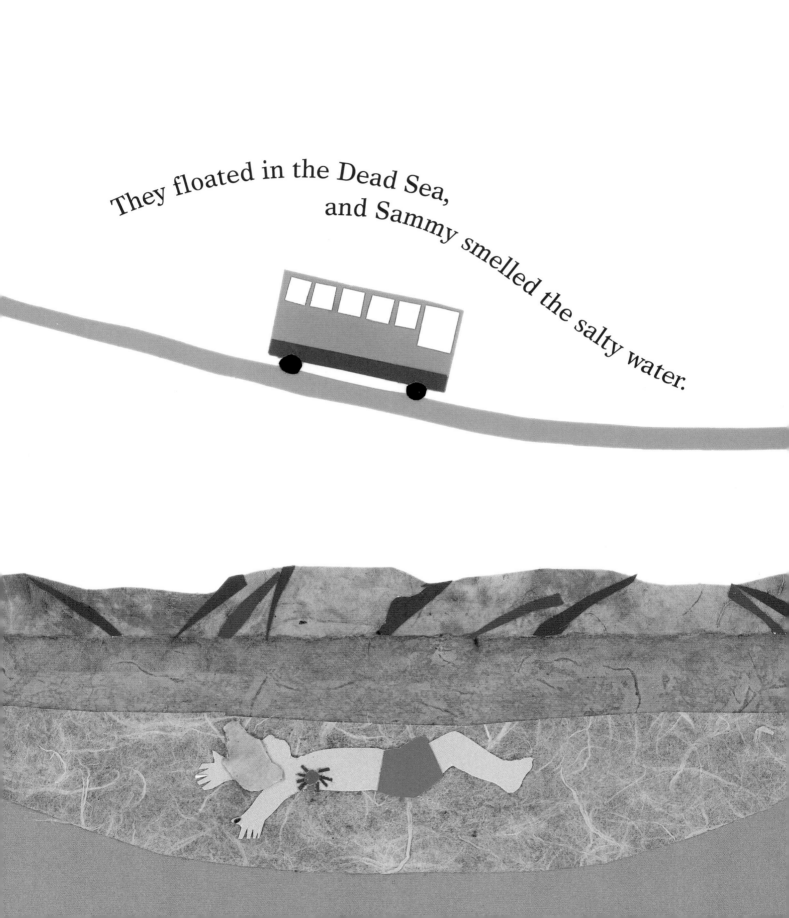

On Shabbat they went to synagogue where Sammy heard everyone wish each other

"Shabbat Shalom!"

"Shalom also means peace," Mrs. Shapiro told Josh. "May we all have a peaceful Shabbat."

Finally, it was time to fly home.

Sammy was eager to see his mother and share his adventures.

When the Shapiros arrived at the house, Josh ran inside and put the little airplane on the couch. Sammy crawled out and shouted,

"Mother! I'm home!"

Mrs. Spider scrambled down to embrace Sammy. "I'm so glad you're back. I missed you so much!" she said.

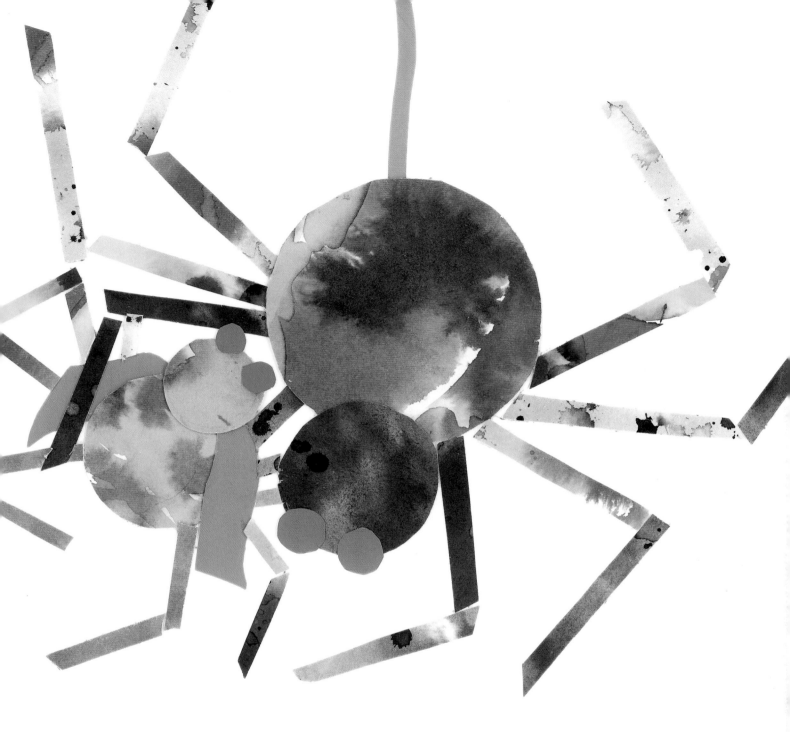

"I missed you, too!" replied Sammy. "I wish you had been with me to smell the sea air of Tel Aviv, hear Israeli music, taste the delicious felafel, see the golden city of Jerusalem, and touch the Western Wall."

"And I have a new word to teach you. Shalom is a special Hebrew word, which means hello, goodbye, and peace." Sammy rubbed his eyes and yawned.

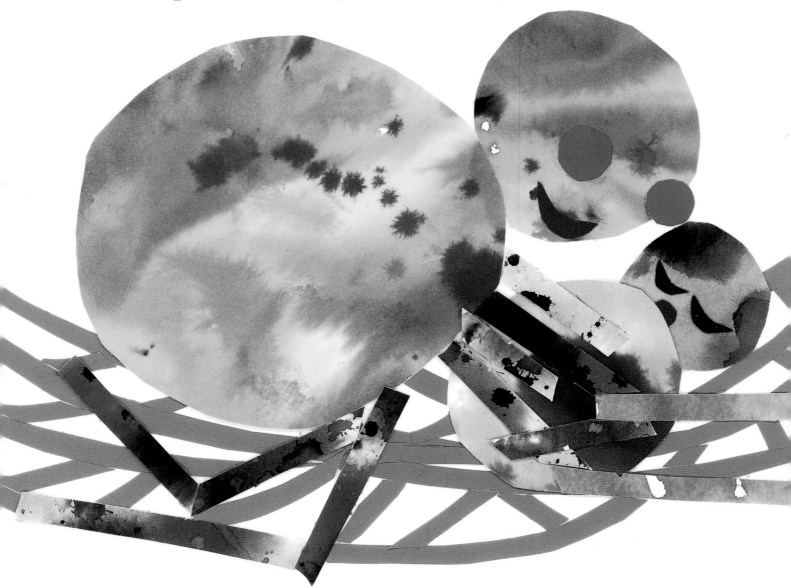

Mrs. Spider gently carried sleepy Sammy back to their web. As she tucked him in, she whispered softly, "Shalom, little Sammy. Hello, welcome back, and sleep peacefully."